A Viking on Turtle Island

A Jormungander Goes Native Short Story

Cathy Smith

ISBN: 9798230824213

Jormungander's Vinland Saga

I may've born in the Far North but I didn't stay there. The Norns think I have nothing better to do than bite my tail in the Northern Sea, but Jormungander, the Midgard Serpent, can imagine more for himself! That's why I journeyed to Vinland in search for new hunting grounds when I first learned of the land.

Mother would've preferred I stay in Midgard. She wants to see it destroyed and the Aesir overthrown. The only reason she accepted the Trickster's overtures was because she thought he was doing an inside job. Loki Laufeyjarson will say anything to get into a comely woman's bed. I used to judge him harshly on this issue since I assumed I had no hope of experiencing the pleasures of the flesh myself.

Technically, I am not a serpent but a jotun. We can assume any shape we please. Though few of us are as prolific as my father. I think Loki mastered this skill because of the "incentives." His taste for strange flesh has almost put the skill of shape–changing into disrepute.

I have a wolf and eight–legged horse for brothers and a half draug for a sister so that should tell you all you need to know about Loki the Trickster's appetites. Though he'll tell you the Olympians in the Aegean Seas are no better than he, "The Olympians have sired monsters too. I think Poseidon changed Medusa into a Gorgon, so he could have some variety though they say Athena did it!"

I find the tales of Father's deeds depressing. Odin's skalds tell cleaned up lays. It could be payback to Loki for doing the dirty deeds he needs to be done, but he doesn't want connected to him. I think Odin stole the mead of poetry to control the Aesir's standing among the mortals and to keep their secrets from their enemies rather than because of an appreciation for literature.

Father benefits from this though he doesn't care about people's disapproval. He wouldn't be able to do what he does if people were forewarned against him. Then again he'd say he can change his shape to disguise himself if it becomes too difficult to go about in public.

He is clever but can never make long–range plans because

he loses interest in projects too soon. Can you imagine how dangerous he'd be if he had patience? I suspect this is the reason Odin has precedence in Asgard. Loki can think quicker than him but there's no reason to fear conquest by the Trickster when you can distract him with a shiny and/or pretty, new toy! To think the Volva says he will be the Jotuns' general at Ragnarok. No wonder we're fated to lose!

As far as, the Vikings are concerned I am a monster with a ravenous appetite, yet I've allowed their vessels to float above me without incident if they have a bard or storyteller on–board. I used to make it a point to devour all who passed my way. That's why their longships preferred to go along the shorelines rather than go out into the open waters. I only let the occasional longship go into the deeper waters so I could get variety in my food supply.

My blood told, and I got bored with floating in the ocean by myself. I had no one to talk to! The whales sang, but I couldn't hold conversations with them. I listened to the seafarers as they exchanged tales of their sea roving. Some had gone south to seas that are too warm for my liking and brought back tales of hiring themselves out as mercenaries in the Mediterranean.

Sometimes they had new tales of Asgard. It's not as good as I could hear in Jotunheim, but I was the only jotun in Midgard's waters.

Or so I thought. One day a captain tossed a gold coin in the waters and intoned, “Let this serve as my toll, Jormungander,” in the tongue my Mother taught me.

I was too shocked to even think of rejecting this offer.

The captain cried out when I emerged from the waters. “What’s wrong? Didn’t I pay you enough?”

His longship was as big as my head and someone in his crew

cried out, “Let's give a blot to Thor!”

The captain was a giant of a man but a runt of a Jotun. He glared at a shipmate who clutched an upside down silver hammer amulet, “I don't care if the Midgard Serpent devours me! The Thunderer will NOT be invoked on this vessel.

This display of boldness made me smile though it looked more like I was opening my maw before I swallowed the vessel and its crew whole.

I hadn't seen another jotun since my time at Utgardloki's court. He offered me the chance to humiliate the Thunderer, and I shifted into cat form to do it.

We got what we wanted and disappeared before Thor could avenge himself, so we celebrated with mead. I drank so much I blacked out, and they were gone when I woke up. No doubt they thought me as dangerous as Asa Thor and snuck out while they could. At least that's what I tell myself...

"I am Ymirling of Jotunheim, and I ask for safe passage for me and my crew within your territory," Ymirling said in our common tongue.

"Isn't this far to go aviking? I thought you sea raiders preferred to prey on settled lands?" I asked in Swedish.

"The monster speaks!" The crew gasped.

"Of course, a spawn of Loki Silvertongue can speak!" Ymirling snorted to his crew on the deck, then he turned to face me, speaking in the Jotun language. "Do you grant me my petition, Jormungander Lokison?

"I want more than gold for payment," I said.

He glanced at his crew and spoke in Jotunese. "Which one do you want?"

What I wanted was information, but I wasn't about to

decline Ymirling's offer, “My price depends on where you're going.”

“I offer you a land whale for safe passage to Vinland,” Ymirling said

“Eh?”

“There is rich farmland across the deep waters. We want to be the first to claim it,” Ymirling said.

I laughed, wondering if a devotee of Father's was playing a trick on him, “If there's rich farmland to be claimed why hasn't anyone done so before?”

“The natives are hostile,” Ymirling sniffed.

I laughed so hard my bulk turned the waters choppy. “So

Odin's precious Vikings can only handle soft villagers!"

Ymirling smirked at my words, "If these are the warriors he fills Valhalla with our final victory is assured!"

I sighed at this," It would be if we were fated to have a competent general."

There was no telling if Father would ever learn the discipline to command an army.

Ymirling grunted at this.

My mood became as murky as the waters I favored, so I changed the subject, "Now what about this land whale you mentioned?"

"Bring Olaf out!" Ymirling said to his first mate.

There was sputtering when the cabin door was thrown open. “What's the reason for this hold up!”

A corpulent trader, heavy with gold, fur and fat tumbled out of the hold. “Ymirling!” was his last coherent word before he squealed like a pig. I swallowed him whole, spitting out the gold jewelry onto the deck. The sailors fought each other over the booty. I smiled as a fight ensued and bodies were thrown into the deep, so I got an even bigger meal without breaking my oath of safe passage to Ymirling. It's not my fault if the seafarers offed each other, is it?

That was my last meal for nine weeks. Prey became so sparse in my hunting area I shrunk. I don't get fat when I'm well–fed, I get extra coils. At this rate my diet would make people mistake me for a whale instead of an island.

I thought it best to scout new territories rather than play games with whalers.

Though I turned into a cat to humble the Thunderer I'm not as skilled at shape–changing as Father. I know how to shift so I can adapt to any waters I find. I may prefer frigid brine but I can swim in warm, fresh water if I must.

The Vikings prefer to travel in the sight of land so I traveled along

Northern shores to see if it could get me to Vinland. I went up, to the west and then forced myself to go down into warmer waters.

I told myself I'd keep traveling as long as I could find food and my various finds spurred me on. There was a seal harpooned by a small man in a skin boat. I devoured them both whole.

Just when a spill of fresh water into the seas repulsed me I came across the richest fishing waters I'd ever seen in my life. Normally, fish are too small for me, but I swallowed enough of a mass to satisfy me. Though it didn’t grow my bulk, it filled my stomach so much I almost spewed out what I ate.

My slow digestion gave me time to watch the area. Much to my delight, whales drifted in, attracted by all the fish. I let them eat their fill. I wanted them to be fat and juicy the next time I was hungry.

The whales are water animals but breathe regular air. That means they didn't need to be choosy about the water they swam in. They went inland to that freshwater inlet.

I snorted. The Vikings work to drive small whales into fjords and these creatures go inland on their own? I was about to let them go on without me, but it occurred to me there may be manflesh inland. I avoid the Vikings' fjords because there's no telling if they'll invoke Thor on me. The one time I swam inland I got stunned by a lightning bolt and woke up with a group of Vikings arguing over the division of my body. There was no telling how long I was out. I would've suffocated if I were a regular sea monster.

Instead, I devoured the quarreling villagers before they could pray to Thor again. I would've stayed on land, but my skin was itching from being out of the water too long. At least I wasn't as helpless as a beached whale; I slithered like a land–based snake back into the water and swam back into the sea.

I didn't want to be in the same situation again, but I didn't want to lose those whales either so I followed them. It was the longest and deepest inlet I've ever seen. The whales loved all the fish they found along the way and I loved them! I picked off the old, the sickly and the calves.

We came to a group of freshwater lakes surrounded by lush woodlands the Vikings would've wanted to clear for farmland. There were long plants in mounds, but I couldn't tell if the mounds were man-made or natural. Plants wouldn't be so abundant if they weren't cultivated, but wouldn't men till the ground in furrows instead of mounds?

I got bored with the whales and fish that weren't seasoned in brine. They were juicy but rather bland. I saw a calf that would make a good parting gift for myself...there was a slithering ripple in the water that moved even swifter than I could!

"Hey!" I cried out as my meal was stolen from me.

That's when I saw her. The pearl–like and delicate scales convinced me the serpent feasting on my whale calf was female. I forgot about my stomach as I was overwhelmed by other appetites I'd never had the chance to indulge in before. She was petite but big enough for my purposes.

Instinct told me I should speak to her rather than take what I wanted by force. “What's your name? Do you have one?”

She hissed at me in, and I made out sibilant syllables though it had odd inflections, “What do you think you're doing on my clan's hunting grounds!”

She advanced on me, so she could envelope me in her coils. Though I could've won the fight, I got distracted. I shivered every time she constricted and squirmed against me to the point I forgot I was in a fight.

She knew and was aware. When her efforts were futile against my greater bulk she swam off. She missed my jaws when I tried to bite her to stay.

I can outrace the Vikings' longboats, but she was faster than me.

We were going so fast I lost track of our surroundings since I was intent only on keeping up with her. I only noticed where I was when she led me to the biggest waterfall I ever saw in my life. She went into its spray and led me into a damp cave.

"Father!" She cried out.

There was a roar. A massive shape fell out of its shadows. I would've been bigger than him in the Northern reaches, but he was my size here! There was no room for me to breathe when he lumbered into my spot. Which was his intent. He meant to squash me flat.

I pushed back and soon he was the one wheezing. I was panting from the exertion but he was more winded by our struggles than I was. His age, experience, and bulk overwhelmed most of his opponents but to me, he was an old man.

Other, younger, serpents were alerted to the struggle and

shouted encouragement to the combat veteran and snarled when I pushed back. Defeating their leader did me no good when there was a nest in this cave!

One of them was about to slither forward to help the older serpent but the she–serpent I'd followed hissed, and he held off. The rest hovered above waiting for the results.

I pressed my opponent until his gasps grew faint and just when I would take a bite from his throat to stop his struggles a familiar voice called out, "That's unnecessary, Young Warrior. You've proved your dominance and won the right to be War Chief of the Serpents from Gaasyendietha."

Just when I was going to ignore their customs and give my opponent the killing stroke my eyes grew dim. The other serpents came forward. *At least I won't feel what's coming*, I thought as I blacked out.

***

Gaasyendietha and I were taken to a chamber to recover from our battle wounds. The womenfolk tended us and the men brought food. I accepted what they brought at first until a hunter looked me over and said, "He'll be nice and plump soon." as he dropped off his latest catch.

"Shh!," she said.

He snickered as he crawled away.

"You're fattening me up?" I sniffed at the food.

"We would've devoured you by now if we wanted to, Young Warrior. Should you fail to recover we'll wait until you're dead ten days before we do so, instead of eating you alive," she said when I spat out the meat.

"You eat the dead?" I shivered.

"We don't allow meat to go to waste," she said.

I laughed until my sides hurt, "Your clan truly is a nest of monsters! I can respect that."

When all my appetites returned the young beauty I pursued told me, "I am Ojisadoh"

"I am Jormungander, the Midgard Serpent," I said.

She frowned, "That's not in the Eastern Woodlands is it?"

"No it's in the Far North."

"You've proven you're worthy of adoption into the Sea Serpent clan but you need to prove your prowess as a hunter before I accept you as my mate."

Father would've told me I should've run while I could, but I had the chance to satisfy all my appetites in Vinland, so I brought back the biggest whale I could find for our wedding feast. A proper trickster would've taken what he wanted and left, but I had nothing better to do. Biting my tail in the Northern waters can't compete with what I have here even if I miss the taste of brine.

Gaasyendietha would've challenged me to a rematch if he were younger. However, he took his demotion as a chance to retire. He protects the hatchlings while the young warriors fight and hunt.

Watching the first batch of eggs hatch made me smile. The Aesir would be horrified to know

I am breeding. Ojisadoh gives me strong sons and bold daughters.

My bride and her clan call me something that comes easier to their tongues. Jormungander, the Midgard Serpent, means nothing in the waters of the Eastern Woodlands of Turtle Island, but its peoples have learned to fear Jodigwadoh, the Great Horned Serpent, War Chief of the Serpents!

Where is Shingebiss?

Ymirling sighed as a little duck waddled onto the ice of the frozen lake. He couldn't help wondering why the duck didn't hibernate like the rest of the animals. He watched it walk to a clump of reeds, pull a few up and make a hole. The duck dived into the hole and disappeared from sight.

An old man had told him he could not claim this land unless he dealt with Shingebiss. He was thinking the old man had lied to save himself a beating because so far that duck was the only creature that braved the elements, and it was silly enough to dive into a frozen lake.

Ymirling was the largest, fiercest and palest warrior the Northmen had ever seen. Yet he had a secret shame: he may be a giant of a man, but he was a runt as far as his fellow frost giants were concerned. This doomed him to lackeyhood in Jotunheim as the best and most coveted lands were owned by frost giants much more powerful and larger than he. He left Jotunheim and went to Midgard hoping to win honor, glory, and lands for himself.

He had followed Leif Erickson to Iceland and Greenland and when Leif's sister wanted to go even further west, he joined her party to Vinland. He did not like laboring under the direction of a woman and he bided his time until they landed in Vinland. Once in Vinland he took the best of their supplies and went even further into the new land. As a frost giant the frigid expanse in the Far North called to him but he stayed below the tree line. There was a bitter winter in the land during his travels but he was a frost giant and that was how he liked it. He followed the longest river he'd ever seen in his life until he finally came to a series of large lakes. He made his way up to the topmost region of the lakes.

Game was plentiful, and he flourished in the frigid land. "A frost giant could grow large here," Ymirling looked at the land in satisfaction. The only drawback he could see was that there were no cultivated farmlands for him to wrest from weaker men. He would have to do all the work of clearing the land himself. "The only thing I have to conquer here is the elements, but that is nothing to Ymirling of Jotunheim."

The wind seemed to blow harder as if taking up Ymirling's challenge. It continued to blow for hours on end but Ymirling trudged on, regardless. When the drifting snow affected his sight, Ymirling finally paused. As a frost giant he did not care about finding shelter in this storm, but there was no point continuing if he did not understand where the best place to go was. When he stopped again, there was laughter.

Spirits take on the language of the men of the land they are in, but they have ways of understanding each other. It took little knowledge of this spirit's language for Ymirling to know he was being mocked. “Who dares mock Ymirling of Jotunheim? Face me like a man if you dare!”

An old man with white hair and white leather clothes appeared before him. Ymirling glared at the old man in disdain, “There is no glory in besting a decrepit old man but if you insist on testing my patience, I’ll still deal with you.”

“I am Kabihona’kan, the spirit of winter, Young One.”

If Kabihona’kan was expecting to inspire fear he was disappointed. “The spirit? You mean there is only one spirit of winter in these parts?"

Kabihona'kan looked at the large, blond giant of a man before him. He understood that Ymirling wasn't a human. "One is all that is needed."

Ymirling dropped his human guise and towered menacingly over the old man in his natural form with his sword unsheathed. "I couldn't agree with you more, Old Man. I am Ymirling, a frost giant from Jotunheim, across the eastern waters in the Far North. I come to win new lands for myself."

Kabihona'kan looked at the sword for one long moment before he said, "Even if you defeat me you can never call this land yours until you defeat Shingebiss."

"Shingebiss. Is he a great warrior?" There would be more glory in besting a great warrior in his prime than this old man.

Kabihona'kan almost smiled, "Only Shingebiss dares to go about the land in the harshest of winters. If you can defeat him, I will recognize you as master of this realm."

"Then I, Ymirling, will find and defeat this Shingebiss!"

He had been looking for over a month and so far, the only creature he'd seen was this silly duck! In his anger and frustration Ymirling blew onto the hole the duck had created in the ice, so it froze over. Much to his surprise another clump of reeds was pulled from underneath the ice and the little duck emerged with a string of fish. Ymirling blinked, “You’re as clever as Loki the Trickster! I'll give you that little duck. You’re a braver creature than this Shingebiss. Is the mighty Shingebiss a coward? I have searched for over a month and seen neither beast nor man in this land but for this little duck!”

The duck paused in its walk and turned to face him. “I am Shingebiss,” it said in the spirit language.

There was a moment of silence before Ymirling erupted in laughter. Shingebiss spoke in the language of spirits and Ymirling knew he was more than just a simple duck. However, he couldn't help thinking a spirit worth his salt would choose a more impressive form. His own folk favored wolves, bears, and giant eagles for natural forms. "You're the mighty Shingebiss? The bravest warrior this land offers?" He shook his head. "How could a little one like you ever defeat a spirit of winter even if he is an old man?"

"Come inside my wigwam and I will tell you how I defeated Kabihona'kan," Shingebiss said.

"You're inviting me into your home?" Ymirling asked. "You're either the greatest fool I've ever met or as bold as Thor the Thunderer but I will accept the offer of your hospitality. I could use a good laugh."

He followed the duck across the lake through snowy fields until they reached the wigwam which ended up being a hovel made of bark. Ymirling assumed human form and was barely able to fit inside. Shingebiss started a fire and prepared the fish for supper. As the fish cooked Shingebiss sang but the fact the wigwam that kept the heat better than Ymirling expected, distracted him from the song.

Shingebiss sang in the language of the land but under it was the language of the spirit and Ymirling heard these words:

"I am Shingebiss and I know how to survive

I can find fish in a frozen lake

My wigwam keeps me warm in the fiercest of storms

Spirits of Winter, you can't freeze me or starve me

You cannot claim the land as yours while I roam it

I am Shingebiss and I know how to survive..."

At first the wigwam was merely warmer than expected but soon it became so hot in the small enclosed space that Ymirling sweat profusely. When it felt like a sauna he panicked, fearing that he'd melt. He ran out of the wigwam to be as far away from the fire as he could get. Finally, his legs gave out, and he collapsed into a deep snowbank.

There was a familiar howl of laughter. If Ymirling wasn't a frost giant, he would've thought it was merely the wind, but he knew it was Kabihona'kan mocking him. He looked up to see the old man's face in the clouds. Kabihona'kan was laughing so hard that freezing rain was coming from his eyes and snow, sleet and hail spittle flew from his lips. Ymirling could not move for days upon end as the old man spat snow, sleet, and hail upon him. Though he was young enough to heal fast Ymirling burned with shame all the while, and it prolonged his recovery. Finally, Kabihona'kan tired of spitting on him and said, "It is almost spring time and Zweegan will be here to claim the land."

Ymirling knew he could not compete with a spirit of spring during spring time, and he left too. He went Far North and then traveled to the East. Eventually he made his way back home to Jotunheim.

Whenever the other frost giants asked about his journey to Vinland, he would only tell them. "I would rather have Thor bash me with his hammer than suffer any more of that wretched land's hospitality!" He doubted he could convince his fellow frost giants that there was no shame in being defeated by Shingebiss, a duck as clever as Loki the Trickster and as bold as Thor the Thunderer.

About the Author

Cathy Smith is a Mohawk writer who lives on a Status Reservation on the Canadian Side of the Border.

She is proud of her people's heritage and also has an interest in the myths and legends of other peoples and cultures and modern fantasy and science fiction which is often derived from past myths and often acts as myths for modern times.

You can follow her at:

Wordpress: bit.ly/2e41qWT

Facebook: bit.ly/2dP3rXd

Twitter: @khiatons

Instagram:@cathy2891

Tumblr: bit.ly/2G3dEjo

Tiktok: bit.ly/3KoGwBf

Sign up to the Cathy Smith-Khiatons-I Write Substack https://bit.ly/4qATMGH to receive news and excerpts of new publications and promotions.

www.ingramcontent.com/pod-product-compliance
Lightning Source LLC
Chambersburg PA
CBHW031933260726
48782CB00065B/321

* 9 7 9 8 2 3 0 8 2 4 2 1 3 *